Para os meus sogros queridos,
Anna Carolina e Walter – ST

For Matt and Emma – DB

Q Quarto Knows

Inspiring | Educating | Creating | Entertaining

Brimming with creative inspiration, how-to projects, and useful information to enrich your everyday life, Quarto Knows is a favourite destination for those pursuing their interests and passions. Visit our site and dig deeper with our books into your area of interest: Quarto Creates, Quarto Cooks, Quarto Homes, Quarto Lives, Quarto Drives, Quarto Explores, Quarto Gifts, or Quarto Kids.

GOOD DOG!

Sean Taylor
& David Barrow

Frances Lincoln
Children's Books

I have all sorts of **brilliant** fun with my owner. He's called Melvin.

Sometimes he likes me **so much,**

he smiles and says,

"GOOD DOG!"

That makes me feel
woo-hoo,
all over!

But yesterday, Melvin left an
extra-delicious-smelling pizza
on the table.

When he came back,
one small slice was missing.

I gazed at him, in a very loving
sort of way. I tried my best to
look like it was nothing to
do with me.

That wasn't likely to work,
when there was cheese on
my chin and tomato
in my ear.

But it was still a sad moment for me,
when Melvin pointed and said...

"BAD DOG!"

Bad? Me??

I felt completely full of unhappy feelings. So I promised myself I would definitely make Melvin smile again and say, 'Good Dog!'

I had a fantastic plan for this.
Sometimes, when Melvin lies
down to relax,

I jump on him, and I give him
a surprise sniffle-snuggle!
That usually makes him smile and say,

"GOOD
DOG!"

So, the next time
he was lying down, I got ready for
a special surprise sniffle-snuggle...

Then I jumped on him.

But I think I chose a bad time.
Melvin didn't smile.
And he didn't say

"GOOD DOG!"

It was a difficult night.

I felt **boo-hoo**, all over!
But I said to myself, "Tomorrow
is **always** another day..."

And, when Melvin came down in the morning, I had a very genius idea! He was in a hurry to go to work. So I **helped him get dressed fast.**

I fetched him socks,

then trousers.

And also pants...

Melvin liked that. He smiled!
And all my instincts told me
he was going to say,

"GOOD DOG!"

I was filled with such a
happy-dog feeling that I did a
whopping wag
of my tail!

And I tipped
over a stool,

which pushed over
Melvin's bicycle,

which knocked
a telephone off
the table

and smashed
a lamp into
bits.

Melvin
stopped smiling.
He didn't say
"GOOD DOG!"

He picked up the broken bits.

He looked at his watch and
grabbed a sandwich. Then he
slammed the fridge door
and went to work.

I was as sad as one lonely tear
all on its own...

until I noticed something.
A packet of sausages had fallen out of the fridge!

Straight away, I made a
plan that would put me
back in a good mood.

First this.

Then this.

Then
yummy!
Yum, yum, yum!

But I had a new thought.

If I left the sausages alone, Melvin would be
pleased with me! I found myself with one of those
life-changing choices we sometimes get.
And I decided . . .

I would NOT eat the sausages!

This put me in a completely difficult situation. I told my eyes to stay shut tight, so I couldn't see the sausages. But one of them kept on opening up!

I went to sleep.
But I had a dream about sausages dancing at a party for sausages.

Even so, I did **not** touch the sausages.

And when Melvin came back,
he smiled. Then he said,

"GOOD DOG!"

It made me feel
whoopy doopy doo,
all over!

I was so pleased, I wanted to
do the **jumping jive,**

the **twist**

and the
hippy-hippy shake,
with my tail!

But I remembered what had happened before.

So I kept my tail **completely** under control.
And everything was fine except...

I was **SO** excited . . .

I did a bit of a wee-wee on the floor.

I looked at Melvin, to see what he thought.
His eyes were closed. And I said to myself,
"Tomorrow is **always** another day..."